We Read
PHONICS ™

If I Had a Snake

TREASURE BAY

We Read
PHONICS™

Parent's Introduction

Welcome to **We Read Phonics**! This series is designed to help you assist your child in reading. Each book includes a story, as well as some simple word games to play with your child. The games focus on the phonics skills and sight words your child will use in reading the story.

Here are some recommendations for using this book with your child:

1 Word Play

There are word games both before and after the story. Make these games fun and playful. If your child becomes bored or frustrated, play a different game or take a break.

I have a match! Could and could!

Very good!

Phonics is a method of sounding out words by blending together letter sounds. However, not all words can be "sounded out." **Sight words** are frequently used words that usually cannot be sounded out.

② Read the Story

After some word play, read the story aloud to your child—or read the story together, by reading aloud at the same time or by taking turns. As you and your child read, move your finger under the words.

Next, have your child read the entire story to you while you follow along with your finger under the words. If there is some difficulty with a word, either help your child to sound it out or wait about five seconds and then say the word.

③ Discuss and Read Again

After reading the story, talk about it with your child. Ask questions like, "What happened in the story?" and "What was the best part?" It will be helpful for your child to read this story to you several times. Another great way for your child to practice is by reading the book to a younger sibling, a pet, or even a stuffed animal!

I liked it when the snake went to school!

LEVEL ④ **Level 4** introduces words with long "e," "o," and "u" (as in *Pete, nose,* and *flute*) and the long "e" sound made with the vowel pairs "ee" and "ea." It also introduces the soft "c" and "g" sounds (as in *nice* and *cage*), and "or" (as in *sports*).

If I Had a Snake

A We Read Phonics™ Book
Level 4

Reading Consultants: Bruce Johnson, M.Ed., and Dorothy Taguchi, Ph.D.

We Read Phonics™ is a trademark of Treasure Bay, Inc.

Published by
Treasure Bay, Inc.
P.O. Box 119
Novato, CA 94948 USA

Printed in Singapore

Library of Congress Catalog Card Number: 2010921693

Hardcover ISBN-13: 978-1-60115-333-3
Paperback ISBN-13: 978-1-60115-334-0

We Read Phonics™
Patent Pending

Visit us online at:
www.TreasureBayBooks.com

PR 07/10

If I Had a Snake

By Leslie McGuire

Illustrated by Meredith Johnson

Making Words

Creating words using certain letters will help your child read this story.

Materials: thick paper or cardboard; pencil, crayon, or marker; scissors

1 Cut 2 x 2 inch squares from the paper or cardboard and print these letters and letter combinations on the squares: a, e, i, o, ee, s, n, k, g, r, t, p, h, m, s, and c.

2 Place the cards letter side up in front of your child.

3 Ask your child to make and say words using the letters available. For example, your child could choose the letters "s," "n," "a," "k," and "e," and make the word *snake*.

4 If your child has difficulty, try presenting letters that will make a specific word. For example, present "n," "i," "c," and "e," and ask your child to make the word *nice*. You could then ask your child to change one letter to make the word *rice*.

5 Ask your child to make as many words as possible that use the vowel-consonant-e pattern (as in *rake*) or the middle vowel combination "ee" (as in *green*). These letter patterns are used in the story. Possible words include *rake, cage, home, hose, rope, green, need,* and *tree*.

Go Fish

Play this game to practice sight words used in the story.

Materials: 3 x 5 inch cards; pencils, crayons, or markers

1 Write each word listed on the right on two plain 3 x 5 inch cards, so you have two sets of cards. Using one set of cards, ask your child to repeat each word after you. Shuffle both decks of cards together, and deal three cards to each player. Put the remaining cards in a pile, face down.

2 Player 1 asks player 2 for a particular word. If player 2 has the word card, then he passes it to player 1. If player 2 does not have the word card, then he says, "Go fish," and player 1 takes a card from the pile. Player 2 takes a turn.

3 Whenever a player has two cards with the same word, he puts those cards down on the table and says the word out loud. The player with the most matches wins the game.

4 Keep the cards and combine them with other sight word cards you make. Use them all to play this game or play sight word games featured in other **We Read Phonics** books.

could

would

oh

there

by

what

should

from

have

I am Bruce.
I wish I had a pet snake!

A cute green snake would be nice!

Oh! There is a snake by the tree!

Or is it a rope?

It is not a snake or a rope.
It is just a green hose.

What if a snake came home
with me? Could I keep him?

I would call him Ace.

He would need a nice cage.

I should keep the cage clean.

What if Ace got huge?!

I would make a HUGE
cage for Ace!

Then, I could get a big basket.
And I would use a flute!

Ace would need to eat.
Snakes like to eat mice.

But my snake should eat rice.

And we ALL could eat an
ice cream cone!

What if Ace came to
meet me in class?

Grace would leap from her seat!

My snake could sleep with me.
So could my three mice.

We would all have nice dreams.

What if my mom saw us?
She would scream!

My mom will never let me
get a snake…

…so I think I will get a beehive!
I like bees!

Rhyming

What else rhymes with snake?

Rake!

Practicing rhyming words helps children learn how words are similar.

1. Explain to your child that these words rhyme because they have the same ending sounds: *snake, bake, cake, flake, lake, make, rake,* and *wake.*

2. Ask your child to say a word that rhymes with *snake.*

3. If your child has trouble, offer some possible answers or repeat step 1. It's okay to accept nonsense words, for example, *zake.*

4. When your child is successful, repeat step 2 with these words:

   Bruce (possible answers: *loose, caboose, goose, moose, truce*)

   tree (possible answers: *bee, fee, free, key, knee, sea, tea, we*)

   green (possible answers: *bean, clean, Jean, mean, seen, teen*)

   keep (possible answers: *beep, deep, heap, Jeep, leap, peep, seep, weep*)

   Ace (possible answers: *base, case, face, lace, pace, race, vase*)

   cage (possible answers: *page, rage, sage, stage, wage*)

Word Families

This game will help your child read words that appear in this story, as well as words that have the same ending.

Materials: paper or cardboard; pencil, crayon, or marker; and scissors

1. Make 6 cards that measure 2 x 3 inches. Print these six word family endings on the cards: **ake, ice, ope, ean, age,** and **eat**.

2. Make 12 smaller letter cards that measure 2 x 2 inches. Print these letters on the cards: **b, c, l, m, r, s, t, w, d, n, h,** and **p**.

3. Place the larger word family cards face down in one pile. Place the smaller letter cards face down in a draw pile.

4. The players all take two or three word family cards and place the cards face up in front of them. The first player then draws a card from the draw pile and tries to make a word using one of his endings. If a word can be made, the player places the card in front of the word ending. If a word cannot be made, the card is placed in a discard pile.

5. Play continues. Players can take a card from the draw pile or the discard pile. Players can make multiple words with each word family card, simply placing new letter cards on top of others.

6. Play ends when the draw pile is empty. The player who creates the most words wins. Mix the cards and play again!

If you liked *If I Had a Snake,*
here is another **We Read Phonics** book you are sure to enjoy!

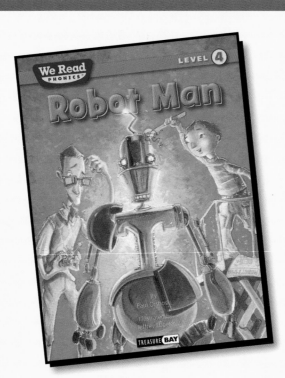

Robot Man

After a boy and his dad build a robot man,
their life is great! The robot man does
all their chores. He even makes them ice
cream treats. Their robot does everything
for them. But then, robot man falls off
the roof and everything goes wrong!